For Elliot,

I loved you before I knew you. You are the very best part of me and my greatest accomplishment. You are my life's wish come true and I hope with all my heart that your dream comes true. I will be the one cheering loudest at your flight school graduation and running onto the stage to hug you tight.

Fly high baby!

www.mascotbooks.com

Flight of Dreams

For more information, please contact:
Mascot Books
620 Herndon Parkway #320
Herndon, VA 20170
info@mascotbooks.com

Library of Congress Control Number: 2018909795

CPSIA Code: PRT0918A
ISBN-13: 978-1-68401-984-7

Printed in the United States

FLIGHT OF DREAMS

BY TANYA THERIAULT

ILLUSTRATED BY JUNICA

He lays his head down
and snuggles in TIGHT.

Surrounded by love, hopes, dreams,
and mum's kisses GOODNIGHT.

"I LOVE YOU," she says,
and turns off the light.

"I'M GOING TO BE A PILOT WHEN I GROW UP," HE SAYS.

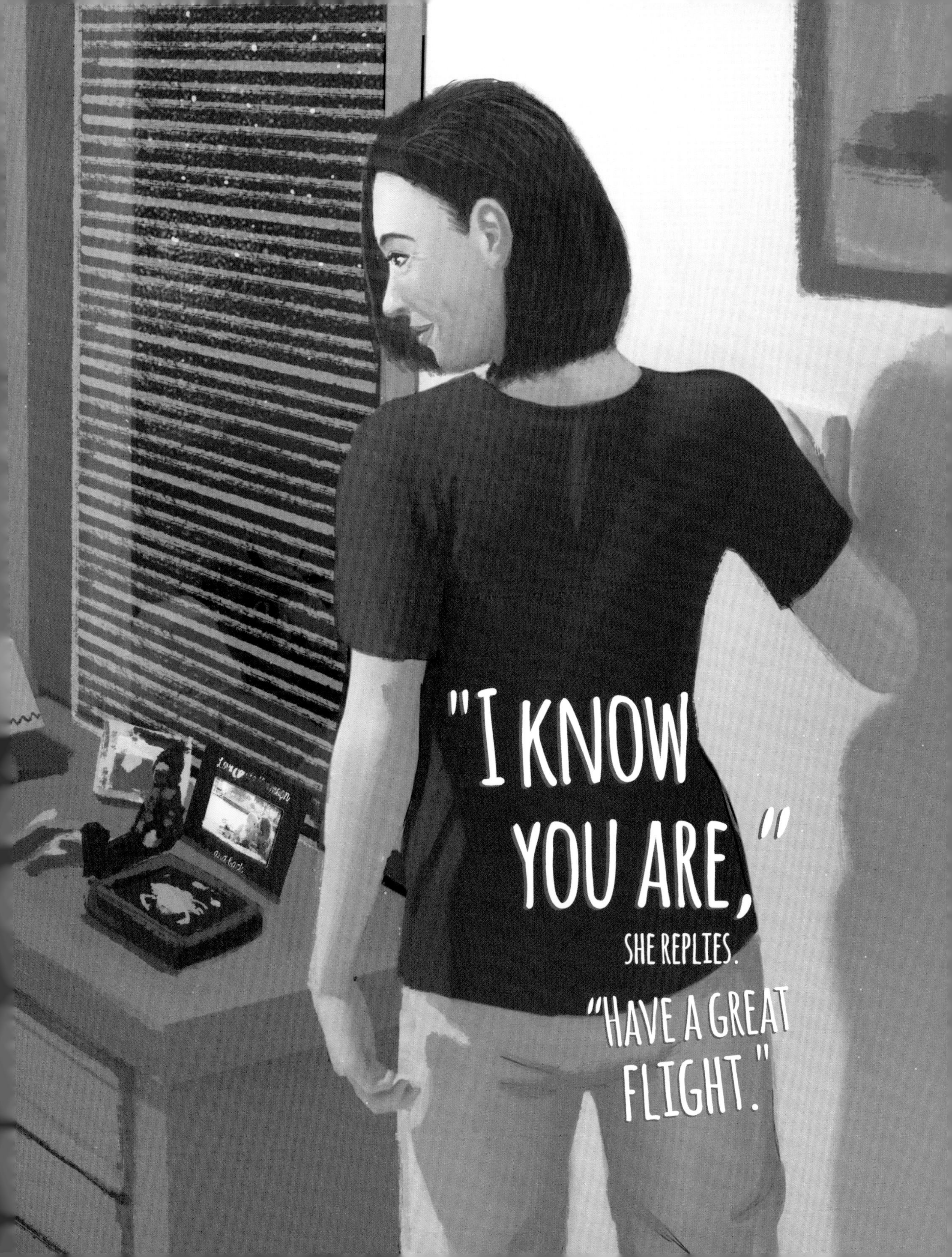

"I KNOW YOU ARE," SHE REPLIES. "HAVE A GREAT FLIGHT."

IN A LITTLE BOY'S HEART
LIVES A BEAUTIFULLY
BIG DREAM—

OF TURBINES AND WINGS,

AFTERBURNERS

AND JET STREAMS.

THE DAY IS DONE.
THE SUN HAS SET.

THE SKY IS DARK
WITH NIGHT.

Twinkling stars
and moon AGLOW—

He is READY to take

FLIGHT.

FLIGHT SUIT AND HELMET ADORNED,
HE WALKS TO HIS DREAM.
HE SETTLES IN THE COCKPIT, CANOPY CLOSED.

HIS BEAUTIFUL SILVER JET—
SLEEK FROM

TAIL

TO NOSE.

ENGINE RIGHT AND ENGINE LEFT—
BOTH FUELED TO THE MAX.

WINGS AUTOMATIC AND THE FLAPS ARE SET.
HIS HEART BEATS FAST AS EXCITEMENT GROWS,

Safety check is GOOD — thumbs up to GO!

His dream
visualizing near.

He soars and spins—
past CLOUDS, MOON,
AND STARS.

Horizon below, mystery above,
EXCITEMENT ALL OVER.

He blasts through the sky just like a

SILVER
SUPERNOVA.

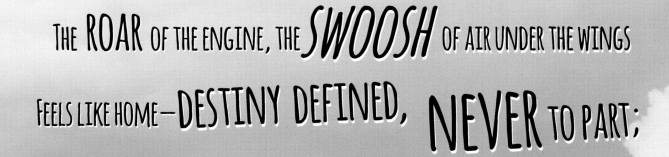

The ROAR of the engine, the SWOOSH of air under the wings

Feels like home—DESTINY DEFINED, NEVER to part;

The RUMBLINGS

of flight playing the music of his heart.

FOCUS, DETERMINATION, PERSEVERANCE, BRAVERY,
DETERMINED TO JOIN HIS DREAM TEAM ONE DAY.

TO HONOR THE BLUE AND YELLOW
A SILENT PRAYER THAT HE ONE DAY MAY.

THE SUN PEEKS THROUGH THE CLOUDS AFAR,
NIGHT'S NEARING TO AN END.
FINAL APPROACH AND BALL IN SIGHT,

Tail hook catches—

smooth as ice and phantom-like.

Delta-Romeo-Echo-Alpha-Mike.

WITH ALL
THAT HE IS AND WILL BECOME,
THE INFINITE WISHES IMPRINTED ABOVE

ARE PAINTING HIS DREAMS

ON A CANVAS
OF LOVE.

IN A LITTLE BOY'S HEART
LIVES A BEAUTIFULLY
BIG DREAM—

OF TURBINES AND WINGS,

AFTERBURNERS

His eyes flutter open as a smile lights up his face. "I'm going to be a PILOT someday," he whispers,

Looking out the window, REACHING FOR DREAMS AFAR.

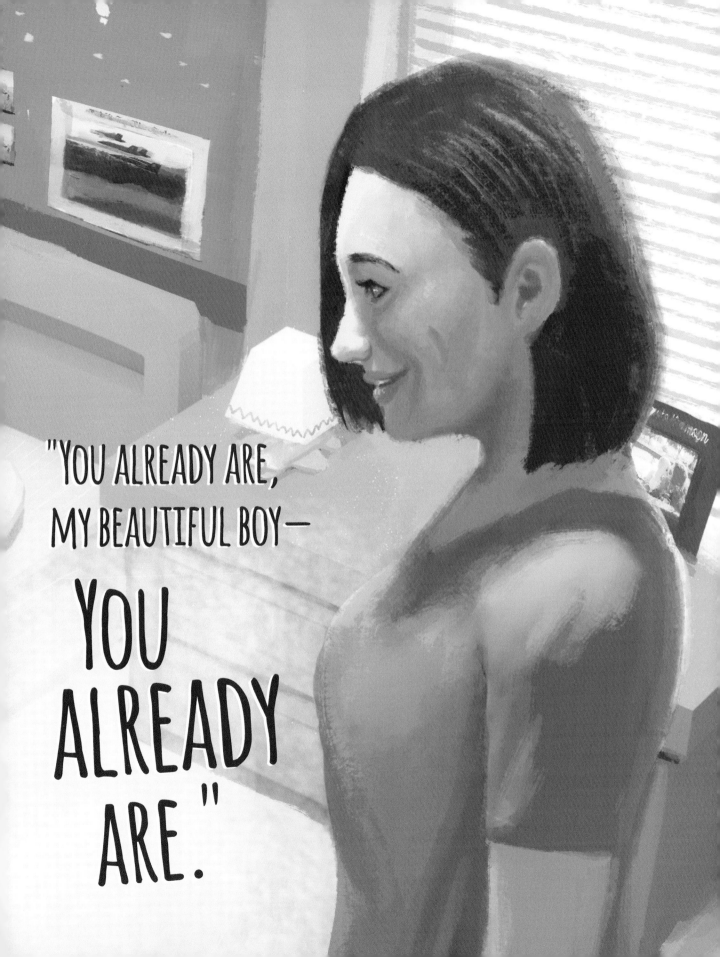

"YOU ALREADY ARE,
MY BEAUTIFUL BOY—

YOU
ALREADY
ARE."

What is your dream?

The mind and dreams of a child are a limitless and wondrous place. Dreams are important. Imagining, being curious, and exploring all help shape who we are and what we will become. Developing passions and learning the value of hard work and perseverance are invaluable to one's future.

In talking to your children about their hopes and dreams, you get to touch a piece of their heart. Listen. Ask questions. Being present and actively listening is very validating. Help your child foster their dreams—research topics, plan trips, and organize enrichment activities.

Dream Big!
Dream Often!
Dream Passionately!

Small children can start by being asked about their dreams—ask your child to tell you about them, act them out in play, draw a picture, etc. "I hope to be a _____ in the future/when I grow up."

Older children can add additional thoughts to their picture about why they want to be whatever it is they want to be and what they love about it.

Tweens and teens can start to look at what steps are necessary to achieve their dream. They can list each step out and what each step would require—now, in one year, three years, five years, etc.

Acknowledgments

National Naval Aviation Museum
www.navalaviationmuseum.org

A portion of the proceeds will be donated to the National Naval Aviation Museum. It is wonderful to be able to have this gem right in our backyard. The museum and staff are wonderful. It is his Disney World— it is the place that has fueled and continues to foster my son's love of aviation and future aspirations to become a naval aviator one day.

SkyWarrior Flight Training Inc.
www.skywarriorinc.com

I would like to extend a big thanks to SkyWarrior Flight School for giving my son the opportunity to experience flight and get a taste of taking the controls. We hope to continue lessons so, in ten years, he can go for his first solo flight. All the flight instructors and staff have been incredible to work with.

Pensacola News Journal
www.pnj.com

A great big thanks to photographer Gregg Pachkowski of the *Pensacola News Journal* for taking the photograph that inspired the story and cover art. Used with permission, copyright 2016.

Special thanks to Joel L. Bouvé, Associate Counsel & Ethics Program Coordinator, -CNATRA, Legal; and Peggie S. Penn, Paralegal Specialist, -CNATRA for helping to obtain the official Blue Angels and Navy trademark licensure.

About the Author

By day, Tanya works with children and adolescents to help them conquer strong feelings, tame poor choices, and reach their full potential to illuminate their future dreams. By night, Tanya enjoys playing the piano, decorating cookies, and learning to quilt.

She is the single mom of a beautifully imaginative, curious, and lovable little boy who dreams of being a future pilot. They live together in the gorgeous panhandle of northwestern Florida with a rambunctious labradoodle and two fish. She and her son enjoy going to the Navy Museum and exploring all the beaches, old military forts, and festivals the area has to offer.